CHRISTMAS HEARTS

THREE ROMANTIC SHORT STORIES

ESSIE POWERS

CONTENTS

Modern Angles   1
Night-Time Water   27
Rumbling Rhythms   55

Author's Note   79

MODERN ANGLES

*W*hen Raina awoke, she could still see him in her mind's eye.

That easy-going smile.

The full, well-blooded lips.

And the high — almost feminine — cheekbones.

Strange . . . one of the strangest dreams she could recall having.

Every bone, muscle and nerve in her body seemed to ache. And, more than anything else, she didn't want to move — didn't want to *do* anything today. On days like these, she considered sending along a bot in her place to work; as was protocol for sick days. So that she might not spread a *disease* about the workplace while still attending in mind . . . if not spirit. But she had already pulled that trick four times this month, taking up a seat at the terminal over in the corner of her one-room apartment and going through the motions; trudging through the office in the bot's body.

She could just tell that the prospect of a disciplinary review was hovering over her; ready to drop at any moment. They would be looking for any sign of what her bosses might term 'lack of commitment'.

And she couldn't lose her job — menial as it might be — her family, out in the countryside, were depending on the credits.

Just the thought of her family sent that wrenching itch going off in the pit of her stomach. She tried her best never to allow her mind to stray — easier said than done — because, whenever she thought about them; about their expansive farm lands which stretched as far as the eye could see, it brought on the same reaction.

The scent of apple blossoms in autumn.

The cackle of geese at morning light.

And then the feel of the fresh, cooling breeze against her skin.

Already, Raina felt as if the tears might begin to flow.

Things were all the worse because of the time of year — because it was Christmas Week; a one-hundred-and-sixty-eight-hour shopping extravaganza. Although Raina loved shopping as much as the next girl, she had never been able to get that excited. There was the fact that her job was intimately tied up with Christmas Week — being in Retail — and then there was the fact that she had never had the credits to spend on the frivolous products which were invariably offered at 'festive' discounts throughout the Week.

Family came first.

Always.

Although, she had to admit, even if it was just to herself, that she somewhat resented her father's financial mismanagement of the farm, consistently turning a loss, year after year; and the way that her mother allowed him to get away with it.

With Raina left behind to pick up the burden.

Not even able to come home for Christmas Week.

To escape the City for just a few days.

With a long yawn, Raina shucked the duvet, allowing it to fall to the wood-patterned tiles of her bedroom floor. She shrugged her shoulders, trying to work out all the tension which'd — *somehow* — built up in her joints overnight.

She sat on the edge of her bed for several seconds before rising to her feet.

As she passed by the full-length mirror which hung to the side of her terminal, she caught a look at herself. She had grown thinner over the past few weeks; and her cheeks had grown much gaunter. And those dark circles beneath her eyes were hardly flattering.

No wonder she hadn't been out on so much as a single date this month.

No surprise that nobody had asked her.

Feeling masochistic, she examined how the washed-out, off-white t-shirt she wore to bed made her look nothing more than skin and bone. It was several sizes too big and had belonged to one boyfriend or another. She had located it in one of her drawers one day when she'd been going through her clothes; working out which ones she could retain and which ones she *definitely* had to chuck away.

Once in the bathroom, and having ditched her t-shirt in a pile on the floor, she found herself thinking again about the vivid dream. She reached up and tapped her temple, bringing her OptiPlant — her optical implant — out of its hibernation mode. She was well versed, of course, about how an Opti-Plant could interfere with the unconscious mind, no matter whether or not it was switched off. And she was fairly certain that her OptiPlant was where the *attractive* male face from her dream had come from.

She ignored the little envelope icon in the corner of her vision, indicating that she had thirty-seven unread messages. With a twitch of the eye, she swished through the various settings for her Opti-Plant, pausing when she reached Activity History.

As she read the log, she saw that the OptiPlant hadn't been active since she'd switched it to hibernation the night before.

Odd.

Really odd.

But, as she well knew, the fact that the OptiPlant had been in hibernation didn't mean that it'd been deactivated. No, it would continue to send and receive signals for just as long as her brain provided it with a natural source of power.

Until she died.

Or until she had her OptiPlant — *illegally* — removed.

She switched her OptiPlant to standby mode, so that it wouldn't bother her unless she received a voice or video call; and then she stepped into the shower.

That face still very much etched on her mind, Raina dressed herself in a silk pair of overalls; the ones with an electric-blue trim surrounding the charcoal-toned material. She wore a matching electric-blue belt about the waist. Over the top, she wore a thick, suede winter's jacket; one which she'd picked up from a second-hand shop . . . not that she would *ever* have told anyone that out loud.

All her remaining credits — after she'd paid off her bills, of course — went into her business wardrobe. She knew how important it was to look good if she was to continue to support her family, out in the countryside. She thought about how things had been different in her childhood, before the City had moved in and bought out surrounding farmland at knockdown prices. They had a level of machination uncontested by any independent operation — such as her family's — and so they had become one of the last farms standing outside the City's influence.

Sometimes Raina couldn't help but shake her head at the irony in the way that her father constantly rallied against the City, and yet — at the same time — how he accepted the same money which Raina's own work in the City brought in.

Perhaps he believed it was a way of sabotaging them through some back door; as if it was some sort of a moral victory to use their own resources against them.

One thing was for certain, by the time Raina's parents finally passed on, there wouldn't be anything to inherit except a decrepit old farm and a mountain of debt.

But she tried not to allow the thought to bother her.

The thought that she would remain here — in the City — alone and near-penniless, for the rest of her life.

She took the first personal transport pod which arrived at her door, despite the fact that she noticed, through the panoramic reinforced glass, that there was a glob of dried-up gum stuck to the plastic seat within. She didn't have time to be picky.

At rush hour, personal transport pods were at a premium, and she was running late for work as it was.

She shuttled along the airways, through side alleys, dipping down below bridges, and then out over the lake which had provided such a dramatic foreground for the City skyline; the image which had featured on innumerable postcards.

She recalled the night she had arrived from the countryside, when she'd alighted from the rail carriage in City Station and felt homeless, lugging all the belongings she possessed in the world, to walk the twenty blocks to see the sight for herself.

Now, though, she might as well have been anywhere.

Most days, she used the transit over the lake as a kind of challenge, to see how many messages she could read and respond to on her OptiPlant from one shore to the next. Her record stood at fifteen. Today, when she surfaced on the other side of the lake, she had got through twelve.

She set her OptiPlant to standby as the grisly, grey — and razor-sharp — building of Modern Angles Incorporated rose up out of the urban sprawl.

Her personal transport, following well-trodden protocols, hummed to a halt at the entrance hall of the building, checked her credentials wirelessly through her compliant OptiPlant, and then, apparently satisfied, opened its door with a faint *whine*.

Raina trod swiftly through the entrance hall of Modern Angles Incorporation, dodging the paths of bots — international visitors and employees who had called in sick.

She briefly took in the Christmas Week decorations; the *enormous*, and surely genetically engineered, pine tree which had silver and gold hanging from its many branches; and a set of lights which sparkled like diamonds dancing up and down.

The air smelled strongly of Christmas pudding and something sweet, which she couldn't quite put her finger on. Only when she reached the internal transport pods did she realise it was the scent of cranberry juice.

Sometimes she wondered just *who* came up with these innovations.

Still, she supposed that it was better than having the entrance hall stink of floor polish, as the hall of her provincial school always had.

She had only just sat down in one of the internal transport pods when she noticed a new message on her OptiPlant. She opened it and scanned it quickly. Filed it into her Spam folder. She gave a slight sigh, mentally replaying the message in her brain, even though it had taken her less than a second to process it and file it where it belonged:

Hi!
I'd really like to get to know you.
Message me back!
Howard

Sometimes Raina felt that the Spam manufacturers — whoever they were — enjoyed having something of a laugh at the expense of City dwellers, and their loneliness. She wondered how many poor saps had been so taken aback by a personal communication among their business correspondence that they had felt no recourse but to reply. Thankfully, Raina hadn't quite reached that point.

And yet, she couldn't help rescanning the message, not with her OptiPlant, only in her mind's eye. The more she thought about it, the more she decided she couldn't resist.

It hardly helped that her pod got caught in traffic coming out of Accounts, and going into her own sector, Retail.

Acting quickly, she fired off a message to her boss, explaining the traffic situation, before digging through her Spam folder, sifting through various warnings which her OptiPlant served her with — advising her not to respond or in any other way interact with anything which had been marked as 'Spam'.

She found the sender soon enough:

Howard Python

The name, at least, didn't sound *completely* spammy, but, she had to admit, the Spam doctors got more and more devious each day in their quest for clicks.

She opened the message from Howard Python, again skipping past her OptiPlant's warnings for her not to proceed. She read the message once more, the textual content. There was nothing which made her think twice, and she was about to leave the message behind, to consign it to Spam forever, when she thought to check over the avatar.

Seeing it in thumbnail, she had to squint to make out the features. She ordered her OptiPlant to maximise the image. And then she was *certain*.

There, in the centre of her vision, he appeared.

The man who had been in her dream.

This being Christmas Week, their boss, Susan Wendings, had three daily meetings scheduled. During the first of these, Raina found herself at a loose end, unable to relate to the current retail 'expert' dressed in overalls with a lurid — almost *clown-like* — combination of multi-coloured polka dots and stripes. Salesmen always felt like they needed to stand out in some way; as if they might not be noticed at all if they chose a sombre, *professional* outfit.

For the first few minutes of the salesman's talk, Raina did her best to concentrate on what he was saying about market saturation of certain products, and the ensuing responses of the consumers, down on the shop floors of the City. But then she found herself irredeemably drifting, turning her attention to her OptiPlant.

To that image of the man from her dreams.

She took in his face once more.

He had neatly cropped sandy blond hair. Hazel eyes. And a strong chin.

It was only the cheekbones which suggested any sort of softness.

And it was that feature which most attracted Raina.

She thought again about the message, about him 'really wanting' to get to know her. And then she thought about the dream. Could this be some new Spam technique?

A way of reaching people even when they were asleep?

The salesman beamed.

Raina forced her attention back onto him.

She noted how several of the other faces

collected about the table wore a similarly dazed look, breaking their attention away from their own OptiPlants.

Making this observation, Raina gave a slight smirk.

She supposed she hadn't missed anything vital.

As someone senior, near the front of the meeting room, questioned a detail within the salesman's talk, Raina turned her attention back to her OptiPlant, and the response she'd been drafting to Howard Python.

She kept it as simple, and clear as possible:

Okay.

Throughout the rest of the day, and the following pair of meetings, Raina kept an eye on her messages. She had sort of been expecting an instant response. Perhaps an autoresponder set up by this spammer, ready to fire off some snaring communication which would put her wonderings to rest forever. Which would only serve to confirm that there *wasn't* somebody out there who wanted to get to know her at all; and that she had just gone and fallen for the most overwrought spammer strategy in all of the City:

Preying on the lonely.

But no message came until Raina was preparing to leave the office.

She flinched when the envelope icon lit up at the corner of her vision. Primarily because, being on the point of leaving the office, she didn't want her boss to somehow finagle a means of keeping her behind . . . there was *always* extra work to be done in Christmas Week; and although Raina had managed to avoid the very worst of it so far, she wasn't so certain that her luck would hold.

But the message wasn't from her boss.

It was from Howard Python.

Meet outside your office?

Raina considered this for a long moment.

Of course, anybody could pull up a citizen's details on the City directory — their approximate residence; where they worked; and their contact details — but implied City conduct often made it somewhat rude to go prowling about the directory instead of making the request personally, or in a message.

All the same, Raina couldn't help but feel intrigued.

This was a man who had appeared in her *dreams*.

And she wanted to know *how*.

She replied, confirming, finished up the last few communications for the day — so that she would be ready for work tomorrow — and then headed down to the entrance hall.

———

Raina stood on the steps which led up to Modern Angles, waiting for Harold. Already she was having a few doubts about her appearance. She had been at work all day, so she was greatly in need of freshening up. She was looking through an article entitled 'Top Ten Mistakes on a First Date' on her OptiPlant. She had only just noticed that the very first tip listed making first contact — let alone *arranging* the date itself — by using information without permission was a definite no-no and was in the process of skipping onto something else when she heard his voice.

"Hi."

Raina turned in the direction of the voice.

And took in Harold Python.

He appeared just as he had in the avatar — just as

he had in her *dream*. All avatars were automatically generated by the OptiPlant, so kept up to date with the person's current appearance. Raina could still recall when that firmware upgrade had been announced and then confirmed; roundly celebrated by politicians and roundly criticised by advocates for privacy. Raina wasn't quite sure where she stood herself on the issue.

But she *was* glad that Harold Python matched his avatar.

He wore a silvery blue set of overalls, which glinted slightly in the sun. He had on a well-polished pair of boots. Already, Raina couldn't help wondering if they hadn't somehow synchronised their outfits.

He extended his hand to her, and Raina took it off him, and shook it.

He had a firm grasp, although he wasn't overtly muscular.

She wondered if he did some light weight training.

For a long few moments, they stood on the steps in silence, before they both — *spontaneously* — broke out in a laugh; the two of them shaking their heads.

"This is nuts," Harold said, "isn't it?"

Raina felt a smile tweak at the corner of her

mouth. And she decided that she had been crushed by loneliness for so long — felt as if she had been the sole living, breathing person in this city for so long, that she should just go with this crazy thing.

"Where'd you like to go?" Raina said.

"I was thinking about somewhere just around the corner. This way."

Raina glanced back at Modern Angles, to the building where she worked, and decided that, really, she had nothing to lose.

Especially with someone so attractive.

Raina had been past the café several times before. It was a place called Bride of Caffeine. She wasn't completely certain whether the name was a pun or some other joke. She had never gone in, though. She had never had anybody to go in *with*; and she'd never quite been one of those people who could sit about in a public place alone. It made her too anxious. If she was to be alone, she preferred to be back at her apartment.

Bride of Caffeine was decorated with green and red tinsel, with a bristling Christmas tree off in one corner. There were portraits — some sketches, some oil paintings — of different brides hanging up all over the walls.

Raina supposed that the owners of the café took their theme seriously.

The air smelled strongly of foaming milk and coffee. Raina hadn't even cast a glance over the glass cabinet which held the various pastries and cakes before she caught their strong *sweet* smell at the back of her throat. It was much warmer in here than it had been outside, and already Raina could feel the heat rising up to her cheeks.

Although, she supposed, it could've just as easily been because of Harold.

For some reason, she found her senses heighten, her ability to be embarrassed raised from just being near him. Like she was afraid of making a mistake.

Harold picked them out a round, walnut-surfaced table over by one of the steamed-up windows. While Harold headed off to go and place their order, Raina sat down at the table. She listened to the *burble* of the crowd; all the people who'd got off work, like her.

Harold brought over their mugs of coffee, set Raina's down before her, and then sat down opposite. He smiled widely, took a sip from his mug, and then set it down. Raina, too, took a sip of her coffee.

It was bitter, and sweet, and milky. And it seemed to restore her senses, to refresh her mind after a long day of work.

"So," Harold said, "do you think this'd be a good opportunity to ask you what you were doing in my dreams?"

Raina felt her chest tighten. Her pulse quickened. A hot flush passed through her cheeks, then a cold sensation through her blood. What had he just said? That she had been in *his* dreams?

Her lips parted, unable to say a word.

Still smiling, Harold took another sip of coffee.

He was waiting for *her* to say something, as if he had just played some masterstroke, and one which she hadn't seen coming.

Well, one thing was for certain.

She *hadn't* seen this coming.

"I . . . uh," Raina began, "I saw you in *my* dreams. That was the first time I saw your face."

"What'd you mean?"

Raina opened her mouth to say something more, but she couldn't think of anything.

How else was she supposed to explain?

"I started having the dreams a week ago," he said.

Raina wanted to jump in and tell him that she

had too, but decided to just take a swig of coffee and allow him to get out his end of the story.

He shook his head, smiling slightly. "The first time it happened, I woke up in a sweat, in the middle of the night, in my apartment, unable to quite believe it." He glanced up. "That I had ever seen such a beautiful woman."

Raina met his hazel eyes.

She felt her heart throb.

Harold continued, "It's . . . I don't know . . . *hard* living here, in the City — don't you think?"

Raina wanted to scream out in agreement, but she restrained herself.

He shook his head. "It's been so long since I've found someone — *just seen the face of someone* — who I thought might be a good fit. Someone going through the same things." He stared deeper into her eyes. "Do you think we're going through the same things?"

Raina held herself back, and then she told him about her family. Even though some little voice at the back of her brain urged her to be cautious, she couldn't help but tell him about how she supported them, about how the responsibility all fell to her.

And how terrified she was about failing them.

Harold just sat and listened the whole time.

When she got through with her story, he shook his head again, and a smile lingered on his lips. "It's uncanny," he said, "your story — *my story* . . . they're pretty much the same, some details here and there — my dad runs a garage, and we live on the other side of the City. But, sure enough, he's stubborn enough to think he can beat the City. That he can beat the *Man*." Harold remained quiet for a few moments, clearly thinking to himself. "You think our Opti-Plants might've had something to do with this?"

For the first time since they had met, Raina recalled her OptiPlant. Looked to its screen on impulse, seeing that it remained on standby.

"Sometimes," he said, still smiling, "I wonder if the standby feature is for the OptiPlant, or if it's for us."

"What'd you mean?"

"Well, I wonder if the manufacturer just put that standby feature there so we'd think our OptiPlants were resting, that we had switched off — when, all the time, the OptiPlant was still churning away, crunching data . . ." his smile widened ". . . finding us dates."

Raina found herself smiling back in response. "This is a date?"

"What'd you think?"

"I think we'd better do this again, just to make sure."

Harold kept up his easy grin as he brought his coffee cup to his lips.

As Raina walked along the street with Harold, the two of them going off to find their respective personal transports back home, she rifled through the screens of her OptiPlant. What she was searching for, she didn't have any *real* idea, but — *somehow* — she caught onto the thought that she might be able to find something that'd either confirm or deny what Harold had said . . . about whether or not the standby feature of the OptiPlant did anything besides *reassure* them.

But she couldn't find any sort of clue.

She did know for certain, though, that *something* had brought the two of them together.

For her, there was no such thing as a coincidence. The modern age had proved so many times — over and over — that fate simply didn't exist.

As Harold helped her into a personal transport, which would take her back to her lonely apartment, he leaned in and planted a firm but tender kiss on her lips. When he drew back, he had a dazed look in his eye.

She wondered, feeling her heart thump in her ears, and with the visor of the personal transport whining its way down, whether he might feel just as love-struck as she did. One thing was for certain, she thought, as her personal transport whisked her around the corner and away from Harold for now. Her apartment might be lonely, but the City wasn't any longer. Not while she had Harold.

And he had her.

In the end she supposed it didn't matter what it was that'd brought them together. For the first time in a *long* while, she'd have some company for Christmas Week. Staying here, in the City, with Harold.

NIGHT-TIME WATER

*N*ela could hear the screeches from the spider monkeys high up in the trees. She trod through the thick jungle foliage, feeling the humidity press against her skin, getting in underneath the loose waterproof clothing she wore, and leaving her with a permanent layer of sweat all over.

Insects buzzed and chattered all around, never ceasing their sounds. She wondered how they managed to keep it up all day and night; but she supposed, as a botanist, it was one of those mysteries which would always perplex her.

Night had closed in about an hour or so ago, and she carried an electric torch snug in her grip, shining a bright white light. Although the pathway which led out to the riverbank was clear, she couldn't quite shift the fear that she would somehow lose her way and be unable to return to camp.

That she would become lost in the jungle.

Whenever she breathed in, she tasted sweetness on the air, as if there might be some fruit-bearing tree always just around the corner. It reminded her of when she had been a little girl and she had wandered about her grandfather's large apple orchard in the middle of the British summer, feeling the sweltering heat coming up off the arid soil. Several times, back in the orchard, she would stop by a tree and pluck an apple off the branch, allowing herself the hidden pleasure of biting into the soft and sweet flesh. Now, though, she was a long way from home; in the middle of the rainforest.

And she was a long way away from that little girl she had once been, too.

In the time since her lonely wanderings through her grandfather's orchard, an academic career had opened out before her and blossomed. It had brought her here. To live among the specimens she had studied for so long in laboratories. To *be one* with the organisms she had always kept at arm's length.

Nela could still taste the sweaty noodles she'd boiled up for dinner. Since she was a vegetarian, noodles had become something of a staple while her *all-male* companions would grill a chicken or else feast on something else slightly more exotic. A couple of times she had caught them, late at night, and after they'd consumed several beers, roasting ants and then crunching on them.

The thought of it made Nela's stomach quiver.

She would stick with her fruit and noodles, thank

you very much, and such modern-world concessions like nutrition — a *well-balanced* diet — could come afterwards.

These days, Nela consoled herself with the knowledge that, while, back home, her family would be feasting on all sorts of unconscionably unhealthy Christmas food: mince pies; chocolate logs; turkey; she would be living a very much hunter-gatherer style of diet.

And there would be none of the usual pressure — the usual *questions* — normally instigated by her grandmother, about her current romantic situation.

Being into her early thirties now, she'd noticed that all the women in her family seemed to have become suddenly extremely interested in her romantic life . . . or lack, thereof . . .

Although she mostly managed to fend off intrusive questions on the subject, she was glad not to have to go through *those* sorts of pressures all over again this Yuletide; and to be many thousands of kilometres away.

In the middle of nowhere.

Nela stalked on through the jungle, her eyes skimming the floor. She did this more out of a strong desire not to miss anything interesting; some specimen which might aid her research, than out of any sort of fear. She had never been afraid of snakes, or spiders, or any creepy-crawlies. She didn't really know why that particular quality had passed her by, or why she was struck with nearly complete nonchalance whenever confronted with such a natural 'horror'. Before the trip out here, Nela had wondered if, the second she actually found herself in the jungle, she might suddenly be struck down with fear. As if just the knowledge of being surrounded by little *beasties* would reduce her to a quivering wreck. Instead, though, she had found that her bravery, if it could truly be called that, had only been underlined by the realisation that most of the animals which lived in the jungle — if not *all* of them — were far more afraid of her than she was of them.

And so she had grown unafraid of walking the jungle in the middle of the night.

She often noticed the looks of fright on the faces of several of her male colleagues, as they would avoid her stare whenever she announced her night-time forays into the jungle; scared that she might ask one of them to come along with her 'to keep her company'.

But she never asked.

And they never offered.

Truth be told, Nela enjoyed her lonely night-time

pursuits out to the river, one of the only times during her routine when she could really be alone.

Up ahead, she could make out the moon's reflection on the river; just about peeping through the low-hanging leaves. She quickened her pace and felt her heart give a couple of hard *beats* in her throat. There was something about the night-time water which had a habit of making her heart tap just *that much* quicker.

Which made her feet just *that much* lighter.

When she emerged on the riverbank, she felt the mud squelch against the sole of her boots. She gazed out across the water, to the bank opposite. Then she looked upwards, to the moon as it hung in the sky. It was so clear, an ivory-white out here in the jungle. The stars were an almost neon-blue.

Never in all her life had she believed that the night sky she would see back home in the city could be rendered hundreds — *thousands?* — of times more clearly once away from the night-time pollution of streetlamps.

But here was the proof.

She had never felt so tiny, so insignificant with her place in the universe as she did now, standing here, on the riverbank, in the middle of the jungle. And yet, at the same time, she felt almost as if the whole universe revolved around this single spot on planet Earth. As if she was the *ant* positioned right in the middle of it all.

She wasn't quite certain what it was which drew her attention from the moon.

When she thought back on it later, lying in her hammock, lightly swinging in the cool, soothing breeze, she would be certain that it had been something stirring in the bushes, on the other side of the river. But when she had looked across the water, there had been nothing to see. Still, it was unspeakably eerie the way the whole jungle had gone quiet — how the insects which provided a constant soundtrack — went silent for several seconds, as if they themselves were wary.

For the first time in the jungle, Nela felt a touch of fear. Nothing more than a stirring of the blood — and certainly nothing stronger than a slight *kick* through her heart. But enough to cause her to curtail her night-time walk, and to return at double pace to camp.

As always, her male colleagues — three of them in all — were playing cards.

The constant *buzz* and *chirp* of insects was only occasionally shouted-down by her colleagues' calls of exclamation or disappointment. And only for seconds before, like a rising tide, the constant noise of the insects would return; almost seeming to become louder than ever.

On their trek out here, into the middle of the jungle, they had brought along camping furniture: collapsible chairs and a table. This expedition was an international affair and her colleagues ranged from places so far flung as Sydney, Delhi and Los Angeles. They were a ragtag bunch, even looking at the matter objectively, and Nela supposed — on some level — she could see her family's obvious concerns about her heading off into the jungle with three strange men.

But — *come on* — this wasn't the fifties any longer. She could stand up for herself. And, anyway, despite the three men all being adventurous types, they were all — behind those biceps and washboard stomachs — unabashed geeky types . . . botanists like her, far more interested in the local flora than romance.

More than anything else, Nela saw the three men as brothers.

She saw that the scientist from LA, Henry and

the one from Sydney, Brett both had a can of — *surely warm?* — beer resting on the table before them. Meanwhile, Amar, from Delhi — a non-drinker — had a water canister.

All three of them glanced up at Nela, gave her a polite smile and a greeting before returning to their cards. And the — *apparently gravely important* — matter of the game before them. Nela paced over to her hammock, concealed behind a vertically hanging tarp she would flip into a horizontal position when it started to rain. It was nice to have a little privacy, and the novelty of sleeping out beneath the night sky — the stars all twinkling down on her — would never wear thin.

Once Nela had brushed her teeth by a stream running close to the campsite, she hauled herself up into her hammock, and draped the thin cotton sheet over her; already thinking about that stirring she had seen on the other side of the riverbank.

It was strange that it would stick out in her mind so prevalently.

Perhaps her senses were heightened because of the full moon and the cloudless night, because of the way the moon acted almost like a streetlight back home, never plunging the jungle around her into complete darkness.

To find sleep, she had to bring the sheet up over her face.

And smother the insects' constant chirps and chatters.

The next day played out pretty much as the rest of the expedition had done.

Nela woke before the others and made herself a quick breakfast from the packet of pre-toasted bread that had been delivered a couple of days ago. Every week, it was arranged that one of the villagers from nearby would arrive with a boatload of supplies, to the riverbank. This being Christmas, though, the boat wouldn't come until the following week, so they had to make do with what they had.

These weekly deliveries were all the contact with the outside world Nela and the others had; and, aside for the emergency satellite phone stowed in a waterproof bag, they had no other means of *making* contact with the outside world.

Nela still recalled, even now, weeks into the expedition, the mixture of excitement and fear she had felt at finding herself in this situation; all at once liberating and *terrifying.* If anything happened to the satellite phone, if anything happened to one of them, the most likely eventuality was that nobody would know for a while. And their expedition wasn't scheduled to finish until next year.

Another two or three months to go.

For the duration of the day, Nela worked near the riverbank. She wasn't sure *exactly* why, although she believed it might have something to do with the stirring she had witnessed the evening before.

What was she hoping to see in the daylight?

Some sort of animal?

She was a botanist, so that was somewhat beyond her remit.

All the same, even explaining away her curiosity to herself, she found that lurking near to the riverbank was irresistible.

She remained there, searching for specimens, but found nothing at all. It was no surprise. For all the time she'd spent by the riverbank, she hadn't ever come across anything that would interest her. Indeed, from her studies so far, she was almost certain of the best spot to focus her search . . . but — for some indescribable urge — she found that she needed to be beside the river.

Just for today.

It was almost Christmas, after all, and she

explained it away to herself that she *deserved* some time off . . . some time away from the daily grind — if it could really be called that.

When night began to set in, and with Nela not having so much as returned to the campsite for lunch, she felt an inexplicable excitement twitch through her stomach. All her senses seemed to tingle. The air grew yet more humid, and the clouds closed in above; looking as if it might be on the cusp of raining. She could smell its slightly stale, almost blood-like scent on the air.

It caught at the back of her throat.

The chittering and chattering about the jungle seemed to lose its volume for several moments, as if even the insects themselves were struck by some sense of reverence for the soon-to-fall rain. She thought about the day before, and how she'd experienced the same phenomenon. She felt both excited and terrified about what she might be about to witness.

That stirring on the bank opposite.

What she had seen the day before.

As the light dimmed around her, she could hear the gentle *crunch* of someone treading fallen leaves. She realised the sound came from behind. She glanced back over her shoulder, in the direction of the campsite, and realised she could overhear her colleagues' voices; returning to the camp. Returning to their card games.

Nela's attention switched back, to the opposite side of the river.

And that was when she saw him.

At first it was like an invisible freezing-cold hand gripped her throat.

Nela's heart kicked a couple of hard beats.

Then seemed to fall silent.

When she opened her mouth, the words wouldn't come.

And — *she knew* — no cry for help would be heard.

Silence pressed on all sides.

Despite the heat surrounding her, she could feel a prickling chill pass over the surface of her skin. Without a conscious thought, she felt her eyes clamping themselves shut. And her mind sweeping her away from the jungle — *far away* from the jungle. All of a sudden, she was back home; back in the sitting room. Standing amongst her family. Her father, mother, and, of course, her grandmother.

Then there were her aunts, some on chairs or lounging on the sofa, others standing up. All of them chattering. And none of them paying any attention to her.

The Christmas tree stood over-decorated and slightly akilter in the corner of the room. Nela had always been raised to celebrate Christmas. It was just the way things were in her blended cultural upbringing: a little of this; a little of that.

The TV was switched on, but turned to mute.

In fact, everything was switched to mute, just as it was in the present.

In the distance, she could smell the gentle waves of the turkey baking in the kitchen. Although she was vegetarian, she enjoyed the odour. There was something soothing — something *familiar* — about it. She could smell the sweet potatoes boiling away, too. Could almost *feel* the gentle, moist warmth of the steam lingering in the air. She could almost hear her grandmother's complaints — the ones which would come later — about the food's stodginess, about how it would 'block' her up.

Nela walked among her family, staring at their faces. Everything silent. Their mouths moving soundlessly. Although she could set one foot in front of the other, she could feel no resistance at all from the carpet beneath her feet. Almost as if she was floating. And, as quickly as the vision had visited itself upon her, Nela felt it fading away again.

Only then did she realise just how much she *missed* them.

Just how hard she *longed* to be back among them.

For a few more moments, that was all.

To soak in nostalgia a little while.

The jungle was returning. The trees and foliage sprung up. No sound, yet, but the jungle had returned. Nela continued to stand stock still. When she looked down to her feet she saw that her boots had disappeared. That her bare feet dug into the reddish-brown mud. It felt a little cold; and she felt impossibly connected to the jungle in a way in which she had never before experienced.

She thought about those times when, away from the camp, she had stripped off her clothes and had a wash in a stream.

But she had felt panicked then; that somebody might arrive and see her at any second, or else that she might happen to turn around and find her clothes were gone altogether and she would have to trot through the jungle stark naked in order to return to the camp.

Slowly, the foreground details became clearer.

She could see *him* . . . what had set off all the images within her mind.

He was a good head and shoulders taller than her; and he stood before her, stripped to the waist, his tight, muscular body exposed. Like her, his body glistened with sweat, from the humidity. His eyes, she could already tell, were a near-paralysing forest-green.

Had he hypnotised her?

He wore a pair of tattered jeans cropped into shorts.

When she turned her attention downwards, she saw that, like her, he wore nothing on his feet.

When had she taken off her shoes?

Had she taken off her shoes?

It made her think about the training sessions they had been given before entering the jungle, before going on the expedition. And how it had been drilled into them that, at all times, they should try to be wearing shoes; or have shoes nearby.

They had no idea what sort of threat they might be facing.

What poisonous creature might be lurking ready to jab them with something that would render them helpless so far away from civilisation . . . or, at least, so far away from a hospital.

Her attention moved back up his body; a body kept in shape by constant action — constant *movement* — rather than a gym.

He had shoulder-length slick black hair and skin the colour of a walnut shell.

And his eyes wouldn't leave hers.

She waited for him to say something; for him to break the constant silence which surrounded them.

But he wouldn't.

His lips never moved.

She only heard his voice within her head.

— *I've been waiting.*

Nela took a step back, shocked, and she felt the sole of her bare foot press down onto something hard; a rough surface. Acting on instinct, she drew her foot away from it sharply. But, although she tried to be quick about her movements, she realised there was no need, that she was slowly — *but surely* — rising up.

Levitating.

She turned her attention back onto the man.

Surprised herself to find that she replied to him within her own mind.

— *Waiting for what?*

— *Waiting for you.*

Nela felt another shudder pass through her body.

For the first time in weeks, she actually felt *cold*. She brought her arms up to her chest and clutched them there tightly, attempting to bring back something of the familiar, humid heat which'd been the dominant feature of her days in the jungle.

As she turned her eyes back onto him, she breathed in a honey-like scent; clinging to him, and seeming to waft over her.

She heard his voice once again, in her mind.

— *Waiting for you to stay.*

Nela woke with a start.

To begin with, she was certain that she was still floating.

When she reached around her, she felt the hammock.

Felt the hammock she had slept in every night since she had arrived here.

Her heart beat hard.

It drummed in her ears.

The sound of the chirruping insects returned to her.

The *cackle* of a distant bird.

She felt the warmth of daylight washing over

her face.

Close by, she could hear shuffling; the sounds of industry.

She turned onto her side. Her mouth tasted stale. The man's honey-like scent still lingered in her nostrils. She glanced down to the area beneath her hammock, saw that her boots awaited her, that — just like always — she had left them where she would easily be able to reach them. So that she simply needed to swivel over onto the edge of the hammock and drop down *into* them.

It took a great deal of energy to move herself out from beneath the sheet which lay over her, but she managed.

Once she'd dropped, busied herself with tying her shoes, she straightened up, feeling almost like an animal, sniffing out its surroundings, trying to determine whether or not there might be an imminent threat lurking.

She couldn't be certain either way.

She glanced off in the direction of the stirring sounds, and, moving quickly, she peeled back the waterproof sheet and peered out and beyond.

She eyed the campsite; their cooking area.

The pots and pans hanging from the cord; a good two or three metres up, where it was hoped they would stay out of the way of less curious animals. Their food, of course, was kept stashed a minute or so's walk to the west of the camp; upwind so as not to attract predators.

She eyed one of her colleagues, the Australian, Brett, from Sydney.

Like always, when he was bumming about camp, he wore a pair of loose-fitting, three-quarter-length skateboard shorts — the sort of garment that an adolescent boy might wear — with a pair of flip-flops underneath. He, like her, seemed to have just woken. Down on his knees, he tended to the camp-fire, so that they might have a cup of tea or coffee with their breakfast.

When he saw her, he flinched, and then glanced around as if there might be someone with her. Slowly, he straightened up, a piece of firewood clutched down by his thigh as if he might be able to use it as some kind of weapon.

"Nela," he said, his voice sounding muffled, as if she had just stepped off a long-haul flight and hadn't yet completely got over the pressurised cabin.

"What? What is it?"

Brett's shoulders rose and fell rapidly. His short blond hair and light-blue eyes seemed so out of place in the jungle. The truth was that, speaking of him as an animal, he just didn't *fit* here . . . at least, he didn't fit as Nela believed *herself* to fit.

"You . . . uh. We've been looking . . . *searching* for you . . . for two days."

Nela's whole body went rigid. "I don't understand. I was just . . ." — she gestured in the direction of her hammock — ". . . sleeping."

Brett continued to stare. Then he snapped out of whatever spell he had been caught by. He blinked several times as if clearing a delusion, and he turned his attention back to the campfire. "We were just worried, that's all. You went away without saying anything. We thought, well, that you might be . . ."

"What?"

"We thought you might be *dead.*"

―――――

Nela's other two companions were equally as surprised as Brett to find her back at the campsite. Although Nela did her best to explain where she had been . . . deciding to tell them that she had simply got lost and wandered back early that morning . . . she saw the way they exchanged glances with one another; the way they seemed to communicate with one another without using words. The same way the man Nela had run into — out in the jungle — had spoken to her.

Once Nela had dealt with the fallout from her disappearance, she managed to extricate herself from the campsite, which was annoyingly difficult . . . though understandable. None of the men wanted to release her from their sight, worried she might go and get lost again; that she might not return this time.

They celebrated Christmas Day with a roast chicken and a small bottle of brandy which Brett had been saving for a special occasion. Nela tucked into her standard fare: a can of baked beans.

Nela felt their eyes on her as she trudged on through the jungle, back towards the riverbank where she had met the man. Where she had first heard the stirrings on the other side of the water. She didn't quite know what to expect; if the man might be waiting for her there, if he might be standing with a gentle smile on his lips, stripped to the waist; urging her to follow.

Speaking into her mind.

But there was nobody and nothing down by the water.

Only the running river current, a few light twigs and leaves being carried along on its surface. There was no trace of the silence, either; constant *chuckles* of birds and *chitters* of insects. Overhead, off in the distance, she heard a peal of thunder.

It sent a shiver dancing across the surface of her skin.

She looked over her shoulder, acting on instinct.

But there was nothing there.

Or was there?

Something caught her eye; nothing more than a few flecks of coloured thread: pink and green and yellow. She trod towards the threads, got closer. When she was a few paces away, she took in the tiny handcrafted structure. It reminded her of a Native American dreamcatcher. The way the thread had been webbed around a series of bound twigs.

She stooped down to retrieve it.

Held it up to the light.

Observed how the day illuminated the frayed thread.

Somebody had left this here.

Somebody had left this here *for her.*

Again, Nela felt a tremor pass through her bloodstream. She got the feeling that someone was watching. She pivoted, determined to track whoever it might be, but she couldn't catch sight of anything — or *anybody.*

Although she felt as if she had come home to the jungle, she knew that those who had lived here their entire lives had grown up knowing the importance of keeping their footsteps light; of blending into the verdant greens and the earthy browns. This was their habitat; as the city had been hers for most of her life.

And it was then, from behind, that she heard his voice.

This time spoken aloud.

"Nela?"

She continued to stare off into the depths of the jungle, to the apparently endless natural labyrinth. If she set one foot in front of the other, and continued to do so, she would eventually be lost forever. Never to be found.

She took care, as if afraid of scaring off a skittish animal — as if the skittish animal *wasn't* her — and turned around.

Somehow, when she took in his dark features this time, when she examined his body — sculpted from a lifetime in and around the jungle — she felt as if it was intimately familiar; as if she knew it better than she knew her own.

And then there were the glimmering, forest-green eyes.

The ones which sensed and considered her every movement.

She looked into them.

They were less brilliant than she recalled, but startling all the same . . . *that* tone of green.

"A Night Elf," he said, as if this explained what she had been thinking.

As if he had *read* her thoughts!

"Our powers only reach their peak during the night-time." He nodded to the river which continued to trickle past, and which was still functioning at full volume — at least to Nela's ears. "This is my place. The place from which I draw my power."

Nela stared long into his eyes, unable to feel herself breathing any longer. The air seemed moist again, and it dampened the back of her shirt. She felt both incredibly hungry and impossibly thirsty. And yet the food was back at camp.

As she stared back into those eyes, the ones which'd seemed so brilliant from the start, she found herself saying — quite without thinking, "Will you let me stay?"

The Night Elf said nothing.

His expression didn't move an inch.

And Nela felt the tension tighten.

She took a step forward, and then another. Soon

enough, she stood before him, and — again acting on impulse, as if she had every right to do so . . . as if his body *belonged* to her — she reached up and ran her hands through his hanging black hair. She felt his smooth, well-muscled neck, and traced her finger-tips upwards, finally reaching his earlobes on either side. Her heart beat harder still. Finally she reached the tips of his ears — *pointed* — of course they were, just as she remembered.

She ran her fingertips across the points before the Night Elf reached up and clasped her hands.

"It's up to you," he said. "Your decision."

Nela's eyes skipped past the Night Elf, and to the silently moving river. Even through the overcast sky, she could feel the warmth from the midday sun beaming down on her back; and she knew that there was no decision to be made.

She locked eyes with him again. "Can this . . . this *place* . . . this night-time water . . . can it be mine too?"

The Night Elf stared back into her eyes. He gave a decisive nod.

When Nela threw her arms about him she knew she had come home.

At last.

RUMBLING RHYTHMS

*M*ichelle eyed the racks and racks of records; all of them marked with discount prices. She wished that it wasn't so, but — *really* — there wasn't any other way.

Her eyes trailed to the front door of *her* shop:

Rumbling Rhythms

She could feel a chill sneaking in around the draught excluder.

Winter was certainly here, and Christmas shoppers bundled through the streets of the London satellite town which she now called her home; all of them wrapped up in their coats and scarves; everybody bustling along business-like with their plastic bags from various high-street chains.

None of them stopped by Rumbling Rhythms, though.

Only a couple ever even peered in through the window. And they were usually children, called away by their parents for dawdling before too long.

It annoyed her to think that she had spent such a long time in investigating the market, in trying to get the branding of her shop *just right* so that it'd appeal to the new trend of record buyers. Those people who still loved the feel of vinyl against their fingertips.

Every day, though, the place was nearly deserted.

She examined the pair of customers who remained in the shop; one, an elderly woman with purple-grey hair wearing a beige-green trench coat; the other, a man dressed in a plain black t-shirt over a pair of tattered jeans.

Michelle turned away in disgust from the man.

She hadn't *ever* been able to understand — let alone *fathom* — that particular trend. She liked to be clean; to *look good.* Just as she thought of herself looking right now: her well-washed, honey-coloured hair gathered into a neat pony tail while she wore a light-pink, strappy top over a pair of close-fitting khaki trousers. And to look at the state of his trainers — scuffed at the toe, the heel . . . and, for that matter, *all* the way around the sole . . . no, it was a lost cause.

She almost wanted to scream it:

JUST THROW THEM OUT!

She ducked down low to the counter, taking some of the strain off her aching legs and putting it onto her elbows. She seemed to have been standing here for *hours*. During the entire day she had made — *maybe* — a dozen sales.

Certainly nothing much beyond three figures in terms of cash taken.

It had been stupid for her to sacrifice her high-flying executive lifestyle for this . . . how had she ever thought that her background in corporate business would make her a success in retail? And especially in a sector which was shrinking at such an alarming rate as music.

She breathed in the cold cup of coffee sitting on the counter before her. She thought long and hard about hauling it into the back room and warming it up again. But she resisted. She would be shutting up shop in five minutes, heading upstairs to her living quarters.

Tonight she was going to have microwaved lasagne. That was a giddy prospect. But she didn't have spare time to lose with anything as frivolous as *cooking*. And it was such a waste of energy to go to the trouble of cooking for one.

The elderly woman gave a cough, and Michelle looked in her direction. She watched on as the woman wheeled her tartan-patterned shopping basket behind her. She opened up the door, glanced both ways down the pedestrianised street, and then left. It slipped her mind to close the door behind her.

Michelle couldn't quite blame her. Most other shops in the area — other shops in the *modern* age — had automatic doors.

With a sigh, she rounded the counter to go and shut the door. On her way past the man in the black t-shirt, she said, "I'm shutting up in a few minutes. Is there anything I can help with?"

It was only then that she took in the man properly.

He had black hair, to match his t-shirt, with a couple of silver tufts glimpsing through his otherwise thick thatch. He was about her age: early thirties. She took in his face, square, and with a little stubble. Other times, she might've thought he looked scruffy, but not now. For some reason she *quite liked* the look on him. He also had bright blue eyes which glimmered. Like a pair of supernovas against his otherwise all-black getup.

When she breathed in, she caught his clean, musky odour, and was already a long way into rethinking her first impression.

He smiled. "No, don't worry about it — I'll come back tomorrow; I'm sure you could do with some rest."

And, with that, and that same smile still stitched onto his lips, he slipped out through the door and into the street outside.

When he shut the door behind him, Michelle was certain she felt a couple of snowflakes brush her cheeks. They seemed almost to wake her up, to stir her from some dream which she couldn't recall ever having.

To bring her back to the real world.

The next day, she woke with light in her eyes. She'd been so tired the night before that she hadn't even thought to pull the blinds. At first she was certain that it was a Sunday; that she wouldn't have to open Rumbling Rhythms until ten o'clock; that she could have a lie-in. Then she realised it was a *Thursday*.

She kicked off her duvet and trotted to the bathroom, dressed in a baggy t-shirt for a band called Nutbolts Spiralling. Since she couldn't recall buying the t-shirt, or even the band itself, she supposed that she'd purloined it from one of her previous boyfriends, though she couldn't quite say why. It wasn't like it was anything special — just a mauve t-shirt with the band's name stencilled in simple white letters across the chest. Maybe one of these days she'd actually bother to Google the name; see if the band was still together.

She was betting they weren't.

She took pains to pick her way through the cast-off clothes all strewn about under her feet. She really did need to think about hiring a cleaner; even just once a week would make a big difference. But it was just another of those things which she *never quite* got around to.

When she emerged from the bathroom, wrapped in a fluffy towel, her hair unwashed to save time, she looked upon her apartment and couldn't help noticing just how unChristmassy the whole place was.

What was more, she didn't feel any strong urge to *make* it Christmassy.

This was her first Christmas without Luke; he had been one of the sacrifices she had had to make when she'd given up her executive lifestyle. The thing was that she simply no longer had time to hang around in cocktail bars after work; she couldn't afford to go out dining in fine restaurants either. Luke didn't seem to understand that she needed to be thrifty now, that every spare penny went into keeping Rumbling Rhythms afloat: into keeping the dream *alive.*

In the end, it had been a mutual separation, although Michelle had been the one to initiate the break-off. She had heard rumours about town; one of her friends had seen Luke with one of Michelle's ex-colleagues. She hadn't asked Luke to explain. Mentally, she had killed off the relationship *months* before.

Why she'd hung on for so long now that the two of them seemed so different, she really had no idea. But there it was . . . she'd always been an old romantic.

But, as she stuck her earlobes with a pair of dangly silver earrings in the shape of Christmas puddings, she reflected that one of the *nice* things about Luke had been his sense of tradition, his sense of occasion. It had been quite a homey feeling to come back to the apartment and find white lights hanging from everything; a Christmas tree in the hallway with neatly arranged baubles. Luke never put together the decorations himself, of course, because, like Michelle, he never had the time. He hired a special *services* company for such things. But it had been a nice touch, and it always put Michelle in the Christmas spirit, without exception.

Now, though — *today* — as she squeezed herself into a pair of black jeans, as she dragged them up to her waist and did the belt one notch tighter than the day before; she had to admit that she felt a Very Long Way Off being Christmassy. Already, her mind had snapped back onto Rumbling Rhythms, and the various tasks which would be facing her the second she went downstairs in the no-nonsense white blouse she had picked out for the day.

The minute she emerged on the shop floor, she spotted the white envelope on the doormat. She bent to pick it up. *Michelle* was written on the front in florid black ink. She tore the flap and slipped a card out from within.

The design on the front was a tasteful — if a little *old-fashioned* — Christmas scene which featured robins and a mulberry bush. She opened the card:

Michelle,
Wishing you a very Merry Christmas.
Season's greetings from Luke and Jasmine

She wondered if she should feel angry, if this was some sort of betrayal. But, even deep down, she knew she certainly *didn't* feel like that at all.

Why should she?

Luke had moved on, and so had she.

Was it just the fact that he continued to leap along at work, earning great money, making a solid future for himself while she scrimped and saved, attempting to keep Rumbling Rhythms alive?

And for what?

Just what was she trying to prove?

A tear sneaked its way down her cheek. She wiped it away then tossed the card out of sight, behind one of the record racks.

———

At quarter to eleven Michelle stood behind the counter with a cup of coffee smouldering away before her. She breathed in the strong, bitter odour, feeling it whisk her back to reality.

Back to the daily grind of keeping Rumbling Rhythms from failure.

Although she had long battled against it, she had finally relented today and chosen to play some Christmas music. She hadn't gone for the standard winter 'classics', though; instead she had put together a rock and punk playlist from throughout the decades, obscure renderings of Christmas songs.

Not that it really mattered, because there was nobody browsing.

Christmas songs had always been something she'd been unable to stand, ever since she was a teenager. It seemed, to her, a level of *twee* well beyond her comfort zone. As a rule of thumb, she never so much as flipped on the radio when it hit the first of December. That was just an accident waiting to happen.

Throughout the remainder of the morning, she ate her way through four or five stale crackers which she had stashed in the back room. She could hardly afford the luxury of venturing out to find a pre-prepared sandwich from a shop nearby, but it was either that or *starve*. Just before she had the chance to slip out and fetch a sandwich, the bell above the door clinked.

Michelle turned to look.

It was the man from the day before.

Today, instead of the black t-shirt, he wore a bulky leather jacket, patches all sewn onto it. Underneath, he had on black jeans. He walked with his hands stuffed in the jacket pockets. A couple of steps into the shop, he glanced over to her and smiled. She smiled back, although she could feel an unpleasant twisting sensation in her stomach and she knew she needed to get something to eat soon. "Merry Christmas," she said, for some reason inspired.

The man turned to examine the record racks. "Merry Christmas to you too."

She dialled down the volume of the sound system, realising the current song was coming to an end. Although the man looked as though he wouldn't be too much perturbed by her *unusual* taste in music, she didn't want to blast his eardrums in.

Noticing the change in volume, he glanced up. "Well, this makes for a change. You should have seen me about ten minutes ago, in the supermarket."

Only now did Michelle realise he held a plastic bag down at his side, filled with items that she couldn't quite make out within.

He gave a shake of his head and flashed his eyes wide. "If I hear 'Jingling Sleigh' one more time I . . . well, it's not going to be pretty."

Michelle felt a warmth pass through her bloodstream, and she knew it had nothing to do with the central heating. If she was lucky, she might be able to get the air temperature inside the shop up to fifteen, or sixteen, degrees.

There was something about this man which drew her attention, something which suggested he wasn't like anybody she'd ever met before.

But she was probably just hungry . . . ravenous hunger did have a habit of playing tricks on her brain.

"Look," he said, those searing blue eyes of his settling on hers, "I was wondering if you'd already had some lunch."

Michelle felt a twitching sensation through her veins. Her heart thumped against her ribs. Her breathing shallowed and shortened. She glanced about the shop and returned to reality. "I . . . I'd love to . . . but I don't think I can — I mean, I need someone to staff the shop while I'm out."

Her stomach crunched, feeling as if she was letting him down. More than anything, she would like to go out for lunch with him. It had been *so* long since she had gone out with someone — so long since she had spent time on *anything* that wasn't Rumbling Rhythms.

The man just smiled, though.

At first she was certain he was putting on a brave face, but then he held up the plastic bag. "Thought that might be the case so I brought a packed lunch."

The man introduced himself as Kieran, and told her

all about how he'd run a record shop himself several years back. When Michelle asked him about what he did these days, he admitted that he'd only just returned home from several years abroad. That he had been working for some multinational company or other, doing something which he was — *surely* — deliberately vague about. He told her how he'd grown bored with the daily grind, with the days at the office, never really seeing anything of the countries he passed through.

And so, just like that, last month, he had quit.

They set up their lunch on the shop counter.

Michelle had half expected to find herself confronted with reams of sausage rolls, pork pies and perhaps a mayonnaise-heavy sandwich, so she was somewhat surprised when Kieran produced several transparent containers which featured couscous, thinly sliced salmon and gourmet oat cakes. She supposed that, abroad, he had embraced something approaching the luxurious lifestyle to which Michelle had also grown accustomed.

But, that said, it wasn't so expensive to eat healthily *and* well.

And, with Kieran, right now, she was doing both.

They'd just about got through with their lunch when the elderly lady from the day before entered.

Michelle felt a slight throb at the base of her gut to think that she had come in the day before, lingered for a long while and bought nothing . . . although she knew that — working in a record shop — she really shouldn't have become so frustrated. After all, if she had been out to make the most amount of money possible then she would never have given up her previous job.

The elderly lady smiled pleasantly. Michelle quickly dumped the emptied plastic packaging from their lunch in the bin beneath the counter. She gave Kieran the flicker of a smile and then brushed her hands of lingering crumbs.

Even if she wasn't making any money at this then the least she could do was *look* professional.

Kieran remained at the counter while Michelle made herself busy, checking over the records, making sure they were neatly stacked.

As Michelle got closer to the elderly woman, she noted how she already had three or four records tucked under her arm, and that, looking down her nose through her thick-lensed glasses, she was gently flipping through a fresh stack with her free hand, apparently ready to buy.

Although Michelle felt the urge to be *helpful*, she

was aware of not crowding her. She didn't want to put off a potential purchaser by seeming overeager.

So, once she'd sorted out all that there was to sort out, she returned behind the counter to stand beside Kieran. She waited anxiously to see what the elderly woman would do next. For some reason, she managed to convince herself that the woman would replace the records, one by one, and then walk out of the shop without buying anything. However, right when she felt as if the elderly woman was becoming self-conscious of Michelle constantly staring in her direction, she approached the counter with her purchases. With a smile, she set the stack down on the counter.

Michelle's hands shook as she scanned the barcodes, and her voice quivered in her throat when she spoke the total price. But if the elderly woman picked up on Michelle's apprehension at all then she didn't let on. She simply dug out her purse, forked out a couple of notes and handed them over. Once Michelle dished out the woman's change, the woman turned to go, her records kept nicely concealed within a brown paper bag . . . Michelle had made a point, when she'd opened Rumbling Rhythms, of wanting to be as eco-friendly as possible.

Hence the brown paper bags.

As the bell tinkled above the door, Michelle allowed herself to breathe a sigh of relief. It felt as if a load had been taken off her shoulders. When she slipped Kieran a glance, and saw him grinning back at her, she couldn't help but give a giddy, girlish giggle.

"Big sale?" he asked.

She gave a shrug.

He nodded to one of the record racks, and flashed his eyebrows. "May I?"

Not having a clue what he had in mind, she granted him permission, and he trod over to the record rack. His eyes just slipped back and forth over the record covers for several moments, and then, like a cat bringing its paw down decisively on a mouse, he yanked one of the sleeves out, and held it up to the light.

When he turned back to Michelle, he was arching an eyebrow. "Do you realise what you've got here?"

Michelle gave him a blank stare.

Kieran tapped his fingertips against the sleeve. "This here's a first pressing, a limited edition — maybe only another five hundred, six hundred, of them in existence." He squinted at the cover in a way which suggested that he might ordinarily wear glasses. "And you're pricing this down at discount."

She slipped out from behind the counter. It sent her hackles up whenever men got into talking about 'pressings' and 'limited' editions. She knew just as much as anybody about record labels and prospective prices. When she arrived at his side, and he handed the record sleeve to her, she turned it over in her hands, looked at the details on the back cover and saw, to her surprise, that he was correct.

She looked back up at Kieran, who was still smiling. She couldn't quite believe how she had allowed that to slip past her . . . it might've cost her a great deal compared to what she had acquired the record for.

"Don't worry about it," Kieran said, "but I think what you might need here is a second pair of eyes, somebody to check your work over; somebody to catch mistakes when they slip through."

She met his brilliant blue eyes, attempting to see some sort of ill-will buried beneath the surface, but she could see none.

"I'll take a look, if you like. I've got nothing but time. No charge."

Michelle glanced back across the entirety of Rumbling Rhythms, feeling her brain skid about, and then she turned back to Kieran, wondering if she could let anyone else into her dream.

Finally, she made up her mind.

They spent the entirety of the afternoon sifting through the record stacks.

Sure enough, Michelle found more treasures which — if stumbled upon by a savvy buyer — would've put her into the red significantly. She thought about the speed with which she had cobbled together the stock for the shop, and how she had gone at lightning pace just so she could get the doors open as soon as possible. Of course certain things had fallen by the wayside — *obviously* — there were issues for her to deal with. But having Kieran around, another 'pair of eyes' as he'd termed it, meant she could get going with her tidying up.

It was nearing the end of the afternoon, and it had long ago gone dark.

She heard a brass band up the road shuttling through Christmas carols, and — for the first time that Christmas — she noted that she had something of a skip in her step. That she felt as if she had something to feel *jolly* about.

It seemed Kieran noticed this too, because, at

every opportunity, he beamed at her, made little jokes here and there as they reordered the stock.

Finally, when the clock on the wall ticked over to five o'clock, Michelle could hardly believe all the work they'd got done during the afternoon. But there was sadness, too, because she didn't want her time with Kieran to end.

It was a long time since she'd felt this close to someone.

As if she just *clicked* with someone.

She went through the closing-up routine — counting the takings, locking up. When she returned to the counter, she noticed Kieran standing there, the card from Luke in his hand, reading the message within. He looked up and flinched. "Sorry. I'm being nosy . . ."

Michelle felt no anger, though. He handed the card to her and she looked it over another time. "Doesn't matter."

There was a long silence.

She cast the card aside then gazed up at him. "I just wanted to say that this has been the most fun I've had in . . . I dunno . . . months?"

He blushed slightly and avoided eye contact. "I was just wondering — if you've not got any objections, or anything — would you like me to help you around the place?"

Michelle hardly had the money to pay for herself, let alone to pay *staff*. "I don't think you'd find it that interesting, and I'm sure you've got better things to do. And you're probably looking for another job . . . I don't want to get in the way."

Kieran smirked. "No need to worry about that — I'll be able to keep myself afloat for a while. And, believe me, I'm not in any rush to leap back into the corporate world." His blue eyes were seemingly bottomless. "So, if you'll *have* me — on a strictly volunteering basis — I might have some ideas on how to turn things around — how to drum up business." He paused for a long moment and then added, "Unless you've got any objections?"

Her eyes harnessed his. The sound of the brass band outside filled her hearing. Her heart beat in time with the snare drum.

Kieran loomed large before her.

His eyes never left hers, even for a second.

And then, when Michelle felt her heart flutter up to her throat, when she believed that — like some sort of Renaissance woman — she was on the cusp of fainting, she felt his lips press *hard* against hers.

She hardly felt the draught as he wrapped his arms about her, drawing her in closer.

When they finally parted, Michelle found herself staring into his blue eyes.

This wasn't going to be such a bad Christmas after all.

As they closed up the shop and readied to go and get a cup of coffee from the café on the corner, Michelle spotted Luke and *Jasmine's* card lying to one side. With a swift motion, she whisked it up, crumpled it into a ball and dropped it into the bin beneath the shop counter.

When she stepped over the threshold of Rumbling Rhythms, and out into the street, Kieran wrapped his arm around her shoulders.

The biting cold hardly registered.

And the music from the brass band filled her ears.

And her heart filled with Christmas cheer.

Thank you for taking the time to read one of my books. If you would like to hear about my latest releases you can sign up for my newsletter here: www.essiepowers.com

Thanks for reading!

Essie Powers

Christmas Hearts
Three Romantic Short Stories